THE FREAKY FACTORY

OPEN HOUSE 2

METROPOLIS SERIES

First published by Beachside Books in 2021.

Text copyright © David Richardson, 2021.

Illustrations by Nigel Venning,
Copyright © Beachside Books, 2021.

Cover and internal design by Nigel Venning.

National Library of Australia
Cataloguing-in-Publication entry

Creator: Richardson, David, author.

Title: Doug and Stan — Open House 2, The Freaky Factory
Written by David Richardson; illustrated by Nigel Venning.

ISBN: 978-0-6489695-2-5. (paperback)

Typeset in Providence Sans Pro.

david-richardson.com.au.

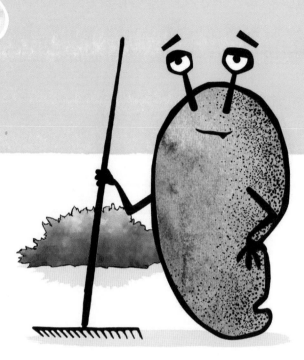

Doug and Stan were sweeping leaves.
So much work to do.
But Stan got really cross
When his brush snapped in two.

'Your phone is ringing,' said Doug.
'Time for a break.'
It was Real Estate Agent Paul.
Doug leaned on his rake.

'Good morning, Uncle Stan.
Some good news to share.
I have a new client
With lots of creative *Flair*.'

Stan listened carefully.
'It's a bit of a mess in there.
But I think it could work.
See you later. Take care.'

Stan hung up and smiled at Doug.
'We will soon be free!
Agent Paul has a buyer.
They want to build a factory.'

'Be quiet,' warned Doug.
'Next door will hear your voice.'
'We must tidy the garage,' whispered Stan.
'We really have no choice.'

'The dark, damp garage?' moaned Doug.
'That will be tough.'
'It has lots of POTENTIAL,' cheered Stan.
'Perfect for making stuff.'

'So much cleaning,' said Doug.
'Work as a team, I assume?'
'Actually, I have to leave.
We need a new broom!'

'REALLY?' added Doug.
'Well don't be too long.'
'I won't,' replied Stan.
'What could possibly go wrong?'

The next door neighbour listened.
'A factory?' she thought. 'No way!'
Then Dotty smiled brightly.
Another chance to play?

She reached for her dress up box.
What would she choose?
So many magical items.
She really couldn't lose.

Doug stared at the brick building
With the old wooden door.
After plucking up the courage,
He got stuck in to his chore.

Old boxes, a dodgy bike
And a gazebo without any legs.
A broken fridge, tins of paint
And a bucket of rusty pegs.

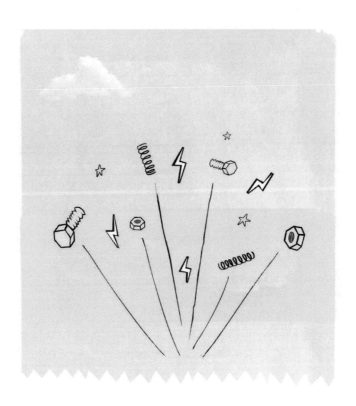

Doug removed the cobwebs.
Spiders scurried away.
Bugs and creepy crawlies.
What a horrible day.

But on the other side of the fence,
Surrounded by her toys.
Dotty was hard at work
Making lots of noise.

Inside her treasure trove,
She found nuts, bolts and scrap.
A spanner, some oil and a remote control.
Ready to spring her trap.

Today she was dressed as a mad inventor.
Her machine almost good to go.
Doug was in for a battle.
Nearly time for the show.

When Stan arrived home,
He stood in the yard.
His mood was very grumpy.
'Why is life so hard?'

Finding a broom had taken ages
But there was no time to DWELL.
Agent Paul turned up smiling.
He had a house to sell.

'Uncle Stan,' Paul cheered.
'This is Rose and Pep.'
But when Stan reached out to shake their hand
He stubbed his toe on a step.

'Owwwwwww!' Stan clutched his foot,
Hopping around like a bunny.
Pep whispered to Paul.
'Is this guy trying to be funny?'

'Rest your foot, Uncle Stan. Sit down and take five. Pep, there is so much room. Make use of the nice, long drive.'

'I disagree!' snapped Pep.
'It's too tight for my truck.'
'Correct, Pep,' added Rose.
'It would easily get stuck!'

'There is tonnes of room for staff,' tried Paul.
'This could be a canteen.'
'The ceiling is too low,' complained Rose.
She really wasn't keen.

'Show them the garage,' said Stan.
'You'll like it a lot, no doubt.'
'Ok,' mumbled Pep.
'Let's check it out.'

But when they stepped outside,
They wanted to scream.
Dazzled by Dotty's magic,
As though frozen in a dream.

Crawling across the lawn,
Towards the garage door.
Was a giant, scary...
Bogey green metal claw.

It raised its two front arms,
Like an angry crab.
Doug hid behind a bush,
Wondering what it would grab.

Then it jumped in the air,
Landing on the garage roof.
Would this be another nightmare?
Doug needed no more proof.

The claw pulled at the tiles,
And threw them in the air.
Dotty flicked another switch.
'This will give them a scare!'

CRASH BANG WALLOP THUMP

So much noise
Made Doug jump.

'Serious!' cried Doug.
'What am I going to do?'
The scrap piled up so high
It began to block his view.

Doug wondered where Stan was.
'Is he still at the shop?
I'll have to do this by myself.
I must try and make it stop.'

Doug sneaked over to the tree
And threw a rotten apple.
DONK!!!! The claw stopped.
'Was there something else to **grapple**?'

Dotty fiddled with her glasses.
'How dare he hit my claw?'
She'd caused so much mess.
Delighted with what she saw.

'I don't care what
These people want to make.
Their big, noisy machines
Will not keep me awake!'

The claw jumped from the roof
And began to chase poor Doug.
Round and round the garden,
Behaving like a thug.

'Go away!' yelled Doug.
'You're getting on my wick.'
'Ha ha ha ha,' laughed Dotty.
'Beware, my claw is quick.'

Then Doug saw the camera,
Perched on its back.
He grabbed a big stick
And gave the pile of junk a whack.

The claw closed in.
Who would win this squabble?
Doug struck another blow
And the mess began to wobble.

Down came the tins of paint,
Turning the claw white.
The wind blew the gazebo,
Like a giant kite.

But then it floated downwards,
Narrowly missing the tree.
Now the camera was covered,
Dotty couldn't see.

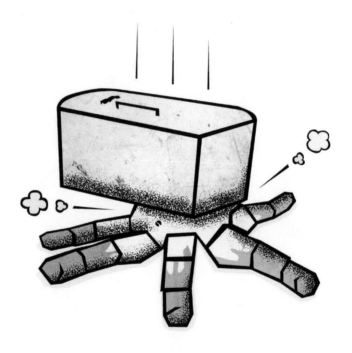

DONK! The fridge fell,
The claw looked proper broke.
Dotty's crazy invention
Was gone in a puff of smoke.

Doug coughed and spluttered,
Then the grey air cleared.
He looked around the garden,
It was no longer weird.

The garage had returned to normal.
The roof tiles back in place.
Then over by the fence,
Appeared a familiar face.

'Hello Doug,' said Dotty.
Her eyes were twirly twirly
And her massive hair
Was so curly curly.

'Was that another one of your pranks?
It caused a lot of stress.'
'I was taking a nap,' lied Dotty.
'That's why my hair's a mess.'

'Then why are you wearing
such weird eye wear?'
'They're a collectors item,' replied Dotty.
'Actually, they're quite rare.'

'Anyway, don't call me weird,' said Dotty.
'It causes me a lot of trouble.
Don't forget everyone just saw you
Smash a giant pile of rubble.'

'How do you know?' cried Doug.
'You said you were asleep!'
'I may have pressed a button or two,' confessed Dotty.
'Did you hear something beep?'

'You're so cheeky, Dotty Sodd!
I feel as rough as a dog.'
'I'm not living next to a factory!' snapped Dotty
'All that smelly **SMOG**!'

'There is no need to worry
About the lovely Pep and Rose.
They won't remember a thing.
That's just the way it goes.'

The back door slid open.
Stan looked so dismayed.
The buyers were speechless.
They felt so afraid.

Agent Paul tried his best.
'Guys?...... Guys?...... Guys?
There's been a mis-understanding.
Can we reach a *compromise*?'

Pep and Rose shook their heads.
'This place is no good.'
They turned on their heels
And ran as fast as they could.

'I don't believe it,' said Paul.
'I was sure they would buy.
Have faith in me, Uncle Stan.
I'm still your guy.'

Another difficult day.
Stan was stressed to the max
And his big toe still throbbed
Like he'd chopped it with an axe.

But Doug wasn't happy.
'Why so long at the shops?
Leaving me here by myself
Busting my chops.'

'You won't believe me,' urged Stan.
'But I tried ten different stores.
All their brooms had sold out.
Gosh, I hate doing **CHORES**.'

'Such a shame the buyers left,' said Doug.
'The garage was as clear as the sky.'
'Well, I wouldn't sell to them!
They were too fussy for you and I.'

As for Dotty?
Stan wasn't very thrilled
But he had to admit
She was very skilled.

The wind had stopped.
No more leaves blowing.
Doug felt deep inside
A warm feeling growing.

Even though his day
Had gone terribly wrong.
He never gave up.
He stayed really **STRONG**.

Afterall, he had battled a claw
And sent it on its way.
Three cheers for Doug.

Doug relaxed in his chair
Enjoying a cup of tea.
Will their house ever sell?
We shall have to wait and see.

glossary

[glos-uh-ree] words with their meaning

Flair [fl-err] a special talent

POTENTIAL [puh-ten-shul] to have the ability to be better at something

gazebo [gaz-ee-bo] provides shade from the sun

DWELL [dw-eh-l] to waste time thinking about something

grapple [grap-uhl] to tangle or wrestle

wick [wik] to get on someone's wick is slang for annoying someone

SMOG [sm-o-g] a mixture of smoke and fog

compromise [com-pruh-myz] to reach agreement with someone

Busting my chops [bust-ing-my-chops] being very, very busy

CHORES [chor-z) jobs to do around the house

fussy [fuh-see] someone who is difficult to please

STRONG [str-on-g] to show strength of body and mind

DOUG & STAN'S NEXT ADVENTURE

DOUG & STAN

THE SCHOOL OF SCARY ART

OPEN HOUSE 3

created and written by
David Richardson

illustrated by
Sumbal Tariq

FOR SALE

BOOK 3
OUT SEPTEMBER 2021

Stan is looking after his friend's daughter, Jane, although a mis-hap at the art and craft table leaves him with his hands glued together. Feeling helpless, Stan soon cheers up when he receives a text...

Stan read the message.
'WOW!!! This is so cool.
Agent Paul has a buyer.
They want to build a SCHOOL.'

Oh no! A school?

That is terrible news.

Actually, it's EXTRA VERY TERRIBLE news!

Next door neighbour, Dotty, absolutely, definitely, 100% DOES NOT like children and wastes no time lifting the lid of her magical dress-up box to begin hatching a very, very crafty plan to put the Buyer off.

FOREVER!

Does Jane's art and craft project make things worse and how will Doug cope with being very outnumbered?

★★★★★

Don't you love it when you buy a book & you enjoy it as much as your children?! This is a delightful book that is easy to read & excites the imagination.
Bernadette, Australia

★★★★★

The story line in this book is a breath of fresh air! Great content, which makes reading this book to your children interesting and engaging to both you (as an adult) and your children. Even my teenage daughter enjoyed this book. The graphics are really, really cool- this is a great book!
Ryan, Australia

★★★★★

What a fab book with great illustrations. The children absolutely loved it. Looking forward to others!!!!
Nicola, UK

★★★★★

It is amazing and funny. I'm 9.
Danny, New Zealand

★★★★★

My daughter and son (8 and 6 year old) loved this story about Doug and Stan. It's a well written story with fun twists and turns along the way. We can't wait for the next Doug and Stan adventure.
Jamie, UK

Get the inside news
on new releases in the
Doug & Stan series PLUS
stories from behind the
scenes, puzzles, prizes
and more by subscribing
to the Beachside Books
newsletter!

To sign up visit
david-richardson.com.au

Follow on
@dougstanbooks

Printed in Great Britain
by Amazon